Contents

Thank you Irene Liang, my tutor !

About MuChing Chen

The author, MuChing Chen, born in 2013, has been interested in drawing animals for over four years. She has lots of different stuffed animals which are the main characters in her books. Outside of being a student, she is also a scientist, artist, and 5-minute crafter.

Don't Let The Piggy Drive The Car!

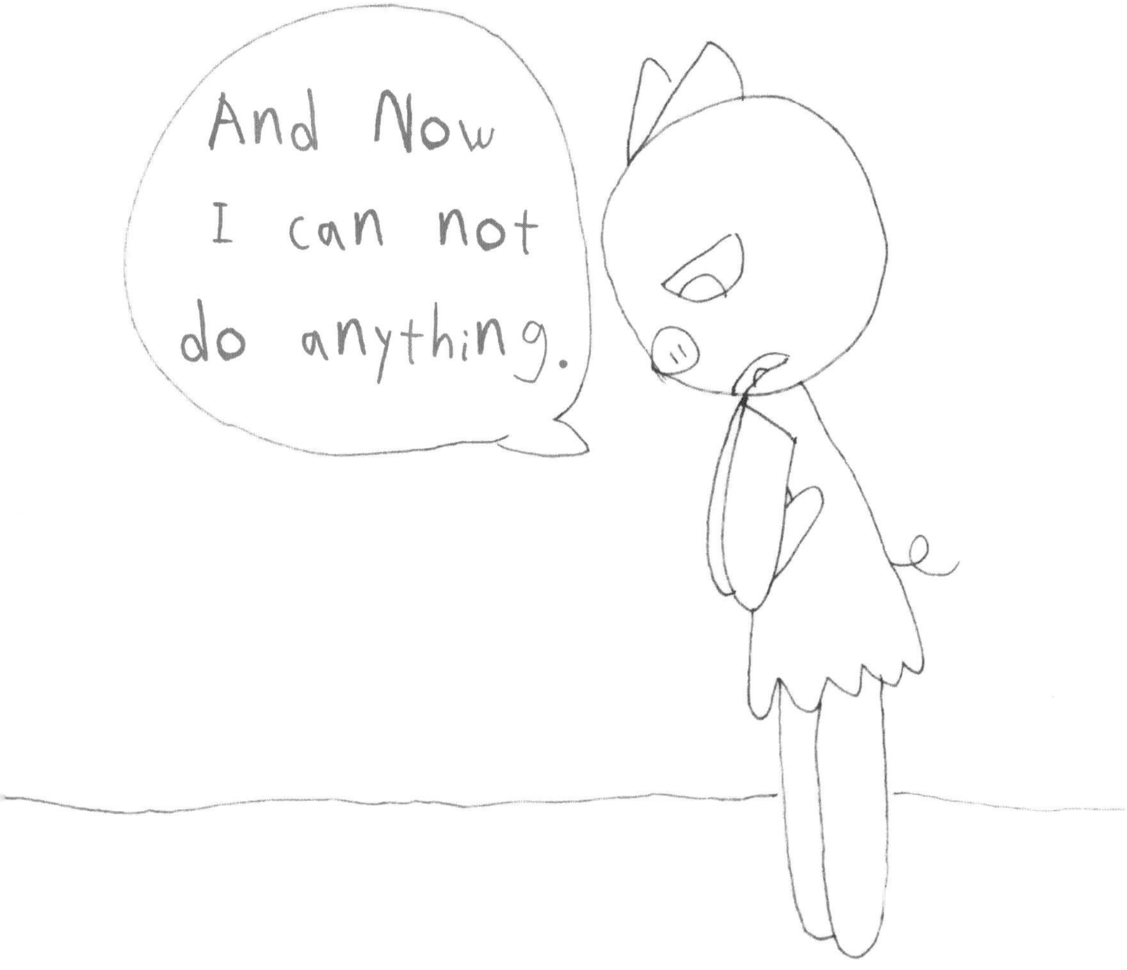
And Now I can not do anything.

8

9

E DRIVE
CAR!

11

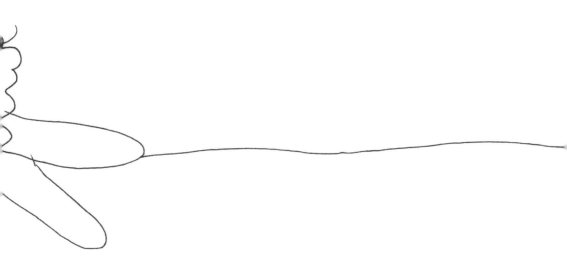

15

19

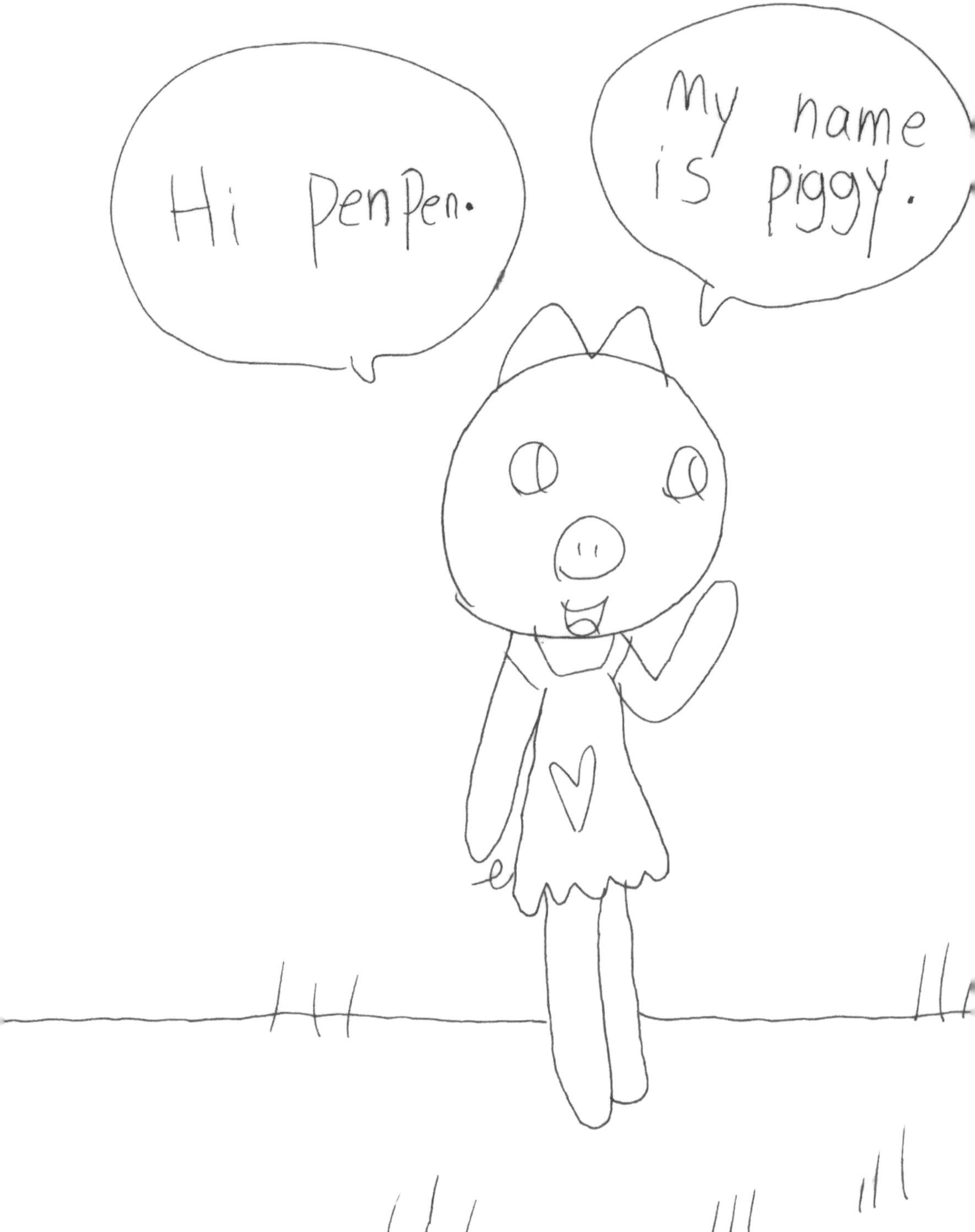
Hi PenPen.
My name is piggy.

FIN.

A Rabbit Who Like To Eat Blueberries.

by MuChing Chen

Mr. Blueberry is playing
with his fruit friends.

Mr. Blueberry and
Rabbet are going
to 7-11 to
buy chocolate
chip cookie.

At the 7-11...

BUT!!
Mr. Blueberry got
LOST !!

>_<

Where
are
we?

Rabbet asked her friends to look for Mr. Blueberry. But Mrs. Strawberry fell and hurt her knees while looking.

When she looked up, she saw
Mr. Blueberry. What a surprise !
Mr. Blueberry is at the park
eating his chocolate chip cookie.
He was never lost !

Mrs. Strawberry got on an ambulance to fix her knees.

Everyone came after Mrs. Strawberry

called about

Mr. Blueberry.

Mr. Blueberry invites his friends
to Rabbet's home again.
Mrs. Strawberry's
knees feel well.

Everyone is at the party and enjoying their time.

FIN.

MuChing

COVID-19

Time Machine

By MuChing Chen

When I am going to school
I see My friend and I
said [Hi] and My
Friend said
[Hi] too.

Then we started to play.
Bitpeg said:do you want
to play tag? Piggy said:yes.

and it's Bitpeg's turns and
she is going to
tag me.

Then it's time up
and we stop playing
then we go to get our
backpacks.

Then Our Teacher
Said: Hello
We Said: Hello

too.

FIN.

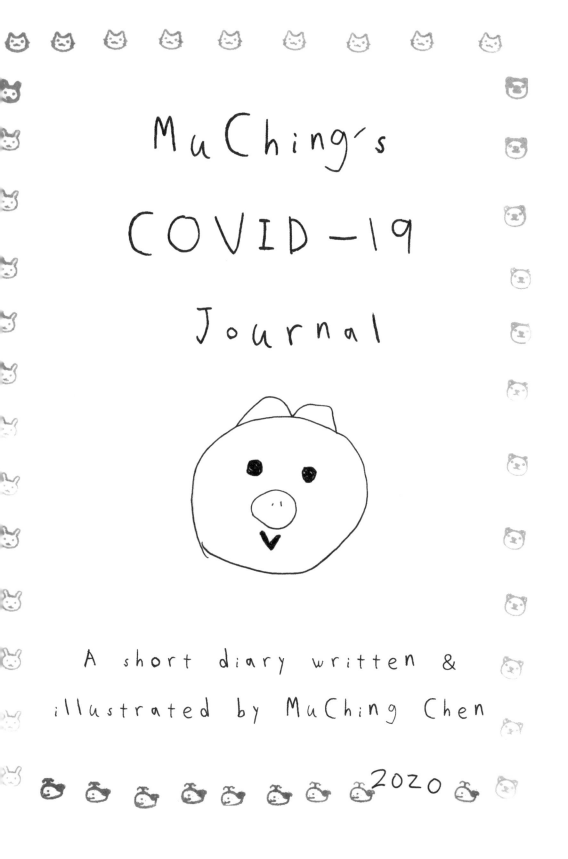

MuChing's COVID-19 Journal

A short diary written & illustrated by MuChing Chen

2020

One day I see so
many people
are wearing mask.

Then Bitpeg said: [Hi]
then I said: [Hi]
and we started to play.

Then we are playing tag again.

and we go to change
Our Outfit.

piggy you look scary Said Bitpeg.
[Yes] Said Piggy.

I hate this !
Said kkim the cat !

I Don't like this Shirt
because it is too cute.
Said kkim the cat.

The we are eating the fruit.

and Our Teachen is helping
us to take a Photo
Then I am Biteing Bitpeg.
Bitpeg Said Ouch!

La La La La ♪♫

Kkim The Cat Sing!

The End

We have more storys than one.

Rabbet & her friends

Printed in Taiwan, Republic of China
For information address:
Elephant White Cultural Enterprise Ltd. Press,
8F.-2, No.1, Keji Rd., Dali Dist., Taichung City
41264, Taiwan (R.O.C.)
Distributed by Elephant White Cultural Enterprise
Co., Ltd.

ISBN: 978-986-5559-82-3
Suggested Price: NT$480